I0601559

The Life of Benjamin Samuel Brasford

Benjamin Samuel Brasford

THE WORK SERIES

https://www.theworkseries.com

The Work Volume I – The Life of Benjamin Samuel Brasford by Benjamin Samuel Brasford

Published by: Intelligent Publishing, Columbia, MD

Interior Design by Benjamin Samuel Brasford
Cover Design by Intelligent Publishing
Editors:
Mary Hoekstra, writeandeditright5@gmail.com
William Bernhardt

Brasford, Benjamin Samuel, 1989 –
The Work Volume I – The Life of Benjamin Samuel Brasford

ISBN: 978-1-7329425-0-9 (Paperback)
ISBN: 978-1-7329425-1-6 (E-Book)

1. Fiction 2. Mystery 3. Suspense

Second Edition, Revised

Printed in United States

Table of Contents

Preface

This is the beginning of a series of books about my own personal journey in life to the point where I am currently. The series will focus on the world through my eyes. A broad array of topics will unfold within this series. Some topics are connected while others are not necessarily. In this reading, I begin with a piece of my childhood and work my way up until the time when I personally decided to accept and live as a Christian of my own volition. This book will reveal some things that you may have never read and it will deliver things from a perspective that you may not be used to.

Introduction

A young boy born in a big city, Hostile, Atlantis, into a loving and religious family, unfortunately was fated to a rough and quite sketchy young life. The family which consisted of the boy's parents, a married couple, and a younger sister. The father made a major career change due to unplanned circumstances, and the family had to move several times within Hostile before moving to a much more rural and slower town by the name of Woods, Atlantis. Woods would be the place where the young Benjamin, called Ben or B, would be reared for the latter half of his childhood, prior to leaving Atlantis altogether to enter what became the roughest and most hurricane-like time of his life. A period which, on the other side brought much clarity, but did indeed leave B with much regret, impatience, anger, and disappointment. Over time, the young lad began to find his way and even found ways in which to move on and let go of the pain and disappointment his past unfortunately left him with.

Mr. Brasford has decided to share with us all his personal story. Ladies and gentlemen, let's get into the life of Benjamin Samuel Brasford, better known as Ben or B.

Chapter I – Childhood

B's family moved several times within Hostile during his youth, which offered very little stability, if any, to a young boy. The mother insured that the children, B and his sister, stayed in church no matter what. Old School Pentecostal Holiness was the brand of Christianity that B's mother's side of the family had espoused. The church location of choice was not within the limits of Hostile, but a good distance away in Coolidge, a much smaller city by size and population. This was somewhat of a journey every weekend to Just Our Time Church, for not only B's immediate family but also his extended family that, too, lived in Hostile. Over time, with the various family moves to different parts of Hostile, the churches, too, would change, though they all had the same or at least a similar philosophy.

B's family started out living within the

walls of their own space. The father and mother both came home every night. Later, the father would choose a job that kept him from being able to come home on a continuous basis in the evenings, a job that would keep him in several states, whether regionally or nationally. He coordinated the shipment of goods via truck and rail. Not long after taking such a position, the family—the mother and children—were forced to perform various moves, even to the point of living with other family members. Finally, after living with various family members, the mother and children could live within a place and community where they no longer had to depend on others to provide shelter. Yet it was not long afterward that they would have to move to Woods, Atlantis, which was hundreds of miles away, to be introduced into a different, slower, and somewhat more stable life that would eliminate all the moving around. It was at this place that B came to an age where he began to develop into a young adolescent and into his young adult years. Because of B's father taking a job that kept him from home quite often, and the type of fathering that his father chose to demonstrate, B would have a rough time developing as a masculine young man.

Chapter II – Adolescence

Ben or B, now living in Woods, Atlantis, had to learn to adapt to a new environment, one that was rural and much quieter, with fewer people and much less to do as far as recreation. A quiet, yet semi-popular young teenager, B got involved in alcohol and marijuana quite early and utilized these substances quite frequently. You see, B was trying to forget something—he was trying to keep his mind off things that happened yesteryear. A nagging yet recurring thought that started too early for B to remember kept plaguing him throughout his early life. It would seem to B that planning was useless. Why plan when you're going to die young anyway? Why hope when it is useless? Why care about anything when no one cares about you? No one took the time, in B's mind, to figure out who B was. No one cared enough to figure out what B wanted, if he in fact wanted anything. From a time, too early for B to remember, these nagging, yet recurring thoughts and feelings continued to plague him. As he got older and older, they got worse and worse. B was not even able to place the context in which these thoughts and feelings were brought into existence.

B, like many other children, went through being clowned and even bullied, verbally and physically within his adolescent years. B never quite learned himself nor understood where he fit or would fit not only in Atlantis but in the world. So, depression and guilt set in, sometimes even to the point of suicidal thoughts and minor tendencies. Self-hate and rejection would become his norm for quite some time. How can any child grow up with self-hate, depression, and suicidal thoughts and minor tendencies in a loving home environment? How can a child growing up in any home and develop this way over time if they truly got the emotional nurturing that they needed?

B was relatively smart in school, but quite lazy and disconnected. B would eventually get his act together, however, aware of some of his earlier family members' failings in school and keep his grades up and finish high School. No aspirations for college, or even a long life, B decided to join the service, the army specifically, and leave home to go on a journey that would cost him much more than he anticipated.

Chapter III – The Service Interruption

The service is commonly thought of as a place where young boys develop into young men. It teaches them skills not only to aid them in their service to protect their country, but also skills that are needed for everyday life. B, not having much with the masculine in his daily life, i.e., seeing it demonstrated at home and otherwise, did struggle somewhat in the beginning. He felt disconnected from his family and friends in the service. This is quite normal. B eventually got used to it and was reassigned to Losem, Now, a city that never sleeps. A 24-hour city that was very different from what B was ever used to. Even Hostile would fail in comparison to much of what Losem had to offer. Losem had casinos, all-night clubs, prostitution. People in general would be willing to do things in this environment that they would not normally do. Yes, even B found himself caught up in some of what Losem had to offer. But B was drawn into some things from a different side, in comparison to what may be considered the norm. In Losem, B found himself very much involved with crowds similar to the type he got caught up with in Woods, Atlantis. Since Woods had little to offer in recreation, the young ones found alcohol, sex, marijuana, and even occasional crime to keep them occupied. Now since the Army doesn't tolerate crime, drugs, and underage drinking, those who decided to get involved in such things had to be very discreet. So, at the young ages of 19 and 20, B found himself being allowed into places that he would not have otherwise gotten into, such as clubs, and because he was part of an older crowd, he would be with older people doing older things.

B, still struggling with that feeling and those thoughts, found himself wanting something more. He had for a time left the restrictions of the religion that he was raised under. He found himself away from his mother and extended family. So B did other things. Those other things were not allowed in the minds of what was acceptable amongst B's family. But B wanted to do what he wanted to do because B figured he was missing something. So B had sex and did other things, knowing that those things went against the teachings of his mother and extended family. But B had a come-to-Jesus moment. He found himself remembering a promise that he had made to "God" when he was around the age of 9. Apparently, B, feeling a certain kind of way even at that young age, promised God that, "If you allow me to live to see age 20, then I will give my life to you." What could have been going on in the mind of a 9-year-old to cause him to make such a promise? What did he hear in church? What did he hear from someone? How did this even come to him? Well, B found himself at that age of 20, thinking about that promise quite often. As it got closer and closer to B's 21st birthday, the remembrance of that promise visited him daily. You see, a year prior, B had begun to weep before he fell asleep at night, occasionally. Throughout his 20th year, B found himself weeping prior to falling asleep at night not only occasionally, but often. B was convinced that he wanted to die. Nothing was really going on in B's life at that time to bring this about. Perhaps this was self-inflicted on his part. He did not understand or know why. His weeping involved wanting "God" to take him out of this place. It appears that nagging, awful, and depressive feeling that he had been visited with over and over for years, had reached its apex.

The military had provided B with a steady job and income. They housed him and fed him. They trained him and provided him with money and time to go to college. No one was harming B. He lived on base in Losem. But no matter what B did, no matter how good things were, B could never lose this feeling. He could never lose these thoughts. And after all of this, B would enter the worst storm of his life, a storm that came with clouds that would remain, just after he was convinced that he would rather die than live.

Chapter IV – Clouds, Rain, Acid, Pain

After having worked in the Army for a little while, B met another Army member. Let's call him BB. BB was a Christian and was not ashamed of it. He delivered the mail where B worked. He began to share his experience and spiritual testimony with B, concerning how Christ had changed his life and gave him a new outlook. Some time later, B began to feel the tug on his heart to get "saved." On a night during the middle of the week, BB agreed to meet with B at B's place, to pray with him to give his life to the "Lord." B immediately felt a weight lift off his shoulders. He lost his desire for so-called bad habits such as smoking, drinking alcohol, having a need and desire to "fornicate," and other things that we learn in church are "wrong." B even shared his "saving" experience with his mother, who was very happy to know that her son just got "saved." Yet the strangest thing took place a few days later. B was invited to BB's church—a storefront church named Soul's Last Stop, a small church with a group of people that appeared happy. Many young folks were membered at this church. B would meet with the leaders of this church, one on one. They began to fill his head with the idea of marrying a young woman who was four years B's senior, who was a complete stranger to him. Let's call her Conflict. B and Conflict would have about a thirty-minute lunch together before the strange event took place. A day or so after the said lunch and meeting with the leaders of Soul's Last Stop, B and Conflict were sitting in the back seat of the leader's vehicle while the man was driving and the woman sat in the front passenger seat. The leaders had now convinced not only B but also Conflict that it was the "Lord" that wanted them to get married. B was so convinced that it was "God" that he didn't want to wait. Conflict never said anything about waiting, one way or the other. Some time later, the leaders took B and Conflict to purchase a marriage license from the court in Losem, and later that evening the leaders performed the marriage ceremony. The marriage was a sealed deal. B would later find out that meeting these people and marrying Conflict would usher him into the worst period in his life. A tumultuous period that would take many years and inflict much pain on the psychological, spiritual, and emotional levels of his life.

You see at Soul's Last Stop, people were encouraged to leave family and friends behind. They were saved now and "better" than all of them. But this also put the leaders into the driver's seat of all the decision making for the members. More specifically, the members who were encouraged to live with them in their own home. The man, Dying, and the woman, Death, were the names of the leaders. A charismatic yet shadowy and puzzling couple they were. If you did not see things their way and make the decisions that they wanted you to make, you were not treated kindly or compassionately to say the least. After all, they were the closest thing to "God" for you. And they made sure that that was understood on a more than regular basis.

When a child grows up with deep-rooted emotional issues, they are susceptible to all manner of manipulation, abuse, and ill treatment, and can find themselves in the worst of situations. This was the period of B's life where the idea of death being better than life seemed confirmed for him.

B often experienced verbal abuse, public and even private humiliation, manipulation, lack of compassion, lack of empathy, lack of sympathy, even spiritual abuse. A very strange and bizarre situation took place. One day while eating lunch at Conflict's place of work, B was sitting at the table in a lunch or lounge room. Out of nowhere, B's head started spinning around beyond his control. Waving around in a circular motion. B caught his head with his hands. Next B began to laugh uncontrollably. Then B began to speak in an unfamiliar language without being able to stop it. Conflict helped B out of the lunch/lounge room to a room downstairs in the building. Then as B was on his knees in this room, his head spun, he spoke the language, and every now and then would stop speaking to laugh. It was seen by Conflict's and B's supervisors at the time. Conflict got B in the car and began to drive B home. B was in the car speaking the language and pointing in different directions. B was helped from the car by Conflict and taken into the leader's home. Dying began to perform an "exorcism" since this was clearly a case of demonic possession. Dying spoke to the "spirits" that were on and in B, asking them their names. The idea was to get the name of the "spirit" to exercise power over it by casting it out. B was on the floor at this point moving around like a snake and whimpering. Whimpering because he had lost total control of his body and thoughts. The little of B that was left was helpless and whimpering. Out of nowhere, Death walked into the home and authoritatively spoke to the "spirits." Some time later, B calmed down and appeared to be back to normal. This same bizarre experience happened once more, the next day, though to a lesser degree. During an evening service, Death demanded that all the "spirits" present show themselves. The idea was to call them out and get rid of them. There were apparently other members who too had "spirits" controlling them. The "spirits" that B faced a day prior began to show themselves again. This time the entire congregation of members got involved in the "exorcism." Finally, later that evening, the "spirits" appeared to leave, or at least change in form. From that time forward, B experienced depression like nothing he had ever faced before. He was never the same. He couldn't do anything right, at least not consistently. He began making some of the worst decisions of his life. He became like a child to his wife Conflict. He effectively was a child. Conflict already had a son from a previous marriage. Now she had two sons. One a toddler and one a newly grown man. A newly grown man without a purpose, care, and without normal functionality in life.

Chapter V - Perilous Times

After the storm of Soul's Last Stop, there were two other churches, not as severe, that were quite similar. These churches, of course, did more harm than good for B, and especially his tumultuous relationship with Conflict. B was still facing the "spirits" that plagued him from the time that he was a member of Soul's Last Stop. Up and down, back and forth, round and round it was for B, especially in his relationship with Conflict. B never learned the game played between men and women while growing up. He failed to realize why his relationship was so perilous and wishy-washy. When there seemed to be peace, chaos was just around the corner. Imagine sleeping next to someone at night, for the better part of two decades, and never knowing what you're going to get. Imagine not knowing who or what you have partnered with, when secrets run rampant and the other party has everyone at their disposal to ensure that those secrets never get out. Imagine thinking that you are doing the right thing, but finding out that you have been duped and manipulated. That you are a utility and are being used for the other party and all you have is your life, which at times seems as if it would be better if it ended instead of continuing as a means for someone else's benefit. This is where B would find himself, yet it took him many years to put the pieces of this complex puzzle together.

B would find himself sharing his story with many people concerning his past and his relationship with Conflict. Whenever key details were mentioned, you could hear a pin drop. But whenever, for the most part, others would respond to the things that B mentioned, they would always take up for Conflict. The game was rigged in favor of Conflict over B. So up and down, back and forth, round and round, like a merry-go-round, B would feel and think, often confused, angry and frustrated. Conflict, as the name implies, was often confrontational, cool, cruel, selfish, bi-directional and even tri-directional. A long and loveless, quite sexless, and non-romantic relationship this was between B and Conflict. B would have to take the blame many times with little to no recourse. Still somehow B managed to keep good jobs and even finish secondary education. B was coerced, earlier, by Dying to leave the military. B had no plan and no guidance from a sensible and supportive source. Somehow, he still managed to make good career choices. B managed to not get into any legal trouble or run-ins with the police. But no matter what B did for Conflict, no matter the sacrifice, no matter the kind gestures, it was never enough. Imagine giving, caring, supporting, and aiding someone but never getting anything in return that doesn't have a dangerous string attached to it. Even those returns with strings were in no way commensurate with what was given.

27

Chapter VI – Discovery

At a time when a transition came, a transition in thought, in emotion, and in circumstance, a light came on out of nowhere. B had a moment where he began to look in the mirror. He took inventory of his life and questioned things. His long-held religion even came into question. B researched and considered things like never before. He even went outside of so-called conventional methods of study.

Sometime later, B jettisoned his long-held position on God, church, and the afterlife. He was finally becoming his own man. He began to talk differently, feel differently, and do different things. This would not make anything easier in his relationship with Conflict, as topsy-turvy as it had begun and remained throughout the life of it.

In one of the unlikeliest of ways, B would become aware of Conflict's past—a past that not only Conflict hid but did many others. B would realize that his analytical mind, the one he always had but never really learned how to use, would help him piece together things. He could piece things together because of his elephant-like memory. B rarely forgot anything, good or bad. Much became quite clear to B. It was the religion, the same religion that he held for the greater part of his life, that he had to tackle first. Once B was no longer convinced that it was the "Lord" that wanted the union between Conflict and himself, it all began to make sense to him. He realized that he had been had.

The source of the information that B was given would even make itself known to him later. It seemed that even within the midst of his "help," that the actual "help" would appear to be yet another trap. B found that when you're too nice, people take advantage of you. They do it because they can. They do it because they want to see what they can get away with. This means that at the end of the day, the only person who really cares about you is, well, you.

B and Conflict would sever their long, contentious union and move on with their lives. B would have to come to grips with his own part played in the downfall of his relationship with Conflict. They were two people that were put together unnaturally, both victims, both having to grow in a difficult situation. In the next discovery for B, he would realize that after all those years of abuse, you don't walk away unscathed. He would have to learn how to deal with his emotions, his mind, his will, and to get his life in order. Ben or B, would meet someone that would help him along the way. Apparently, someone did care about B other than himself. At many times, B didn't even care about himself. Let's call this help DRR or D.

Chapter VII – The Balancing Act and The Brighter and Stronger Future

At a time where the crossroads truly came into view, in walked an opportunity. A fresh start so it would seem, or perhaps just a new way of seeing things so that B could move on. B finally realized that it was time for him to live his own life and make his own decisions. Because of the past, he found himself with much anger, frustration, and impatience. When one has gone through a fire, even coming out of it unscathed as they say, they still pick up issues that will need to be addressed. Life has a way of beating you up on the different levels, i.e., psychological, emotional, spiritual and physical. B began to look at things as a do it or don't kind of thing. He unfortunately allowed a lot of bad behavior from others to plague him. He didn't really know any better and because of his personality, people thought that they could do and say whatever they wanted after a time. But at the end of the day, just because someone may allow something, it doesn't mean that it should be done to them. Responsibility lies on both parties.

Mid-morning, Wednesday, at the city between the metropolises, another gentleman, who had a similar childhood to B's, was sitting in a coffee shop on W Street. He was ten years B's senior. He had an iPad with him and a notepad, writing while occasionally sipping his coffee. D was his name. He was a wise and quite affluent fellow. Unmarried, he had no immediate family of his own, but had the occasional fling or two.

B walked in the coffee shop, got his coffee—black with no cream or sugar—paid for it, and sat at a table near D. D saw B sitting alone while appearing to have something on his mind that was troubling him.

So, D began a conversation with B. "What's

going on? You good?"

B said, "I'm good. Life is what it is at times. Never thought that it would be this way."

"I feel you man. No one prepared us for many possibilities that life could and/or would bring. But think about it. How could they? How could anyone prepare their child or anyone else for every possibility?" said D.

B replied, "You're right, man. So many people bring me cliché talk. They fail to understand my life and past but love to come with generalities that don't even remotely fit my situation."

D, not wanting to get too deep as well as realizing that he had something to do, said, "Alright bruh, I have to run. Here's my number man. Hit me up sometime and we can chop it up."

B replied, "Sure man, I appreciate that."

They both gave each other dap and D left.

On a Saturday night in the rumbling city, let's call it the "Hot District," B was chilling with some of his boys at club "Hotness," after one of them bought the group of fellas a round of drinks. B would go out occasionally to hang with friends and meet a girl here and there.

This particular night, D was present in "Hotness." D had two women seated with him, one a fling of his and the other a potential fling, though D and this young lady kept it hush. He noticed B at the bar alone, waiting for a drink. D got up and greeted B. "Yo, what's up man? You come here from time to time?"

B replied, "Naw, man. Actually, this is my first time here. Hanging with my boys, man, drinking and hoping I see a girl that fits my liking."

D said, "Bruh, you don't see nothing in here that you don't like? Bruh, I got two of them now. They both off limits though." D chuckled after having said that. "But seriously man, there are some hot ones in here, man. You must be an introvert, huh?"

B said, "I am. It's been a long time since I've been in the game. I was married for a minute."

D said, "Yeah, well, that marriage shit is for the birds as far as I am concerned. But I understand. Yo, what you doing tomorrow man?"

B replied, "Nothing, man. Chilling, you know? Probably going to clean up and relax. Get ready for work Monday morning."

D said, "Yeah that 9-to-5 hustle. I gave up on that a long time ago. I've been working for myself obtaining several different methods to bring in money. I come and go as I please, man."

B stated, "Yeah, I would love that, man, but I don't know anyone really doing anything."

D said, "Bruh, hit me up sometime. We can talk about it and I'll see what I can do for you."

B said, "Cool, man. Will do."

D stated, "Alright man, get you some numbers and see if you can take a girl home tonight, my dude. I'm taking one home tonight, and the other one I'll get at soon." They both gave each other dap. D went back to his two lady guests, and B found his boys.

After a few weeks, on a Thursday, B was in a bookstore, "Thoroughread," going through the aisles looking for intellectual and thought-provoking subjects such as spiritualism, history, and philosophy. As B went to the history section, he saw D thumbing through a book on ancient Egypt. "What's up, man?"

D replied, "Damn, man, I swear we keep accidentally or perhaps fatefully running into each other."

B said, "I suppose, man. I've been meaning to get at you, but I've been hanging tough with my girlfriend."

D said, "I hear you with that girlfriend shit, man. Not putting you down, but as a businessman, that dating and courting takes up a lot of time and effort. And, if you don't get an understanding woman as your girl, good luck with that shit. A man needs to have a passion and a drive to do something. To be something. Some of these women say that they want that but I've seen many try to sabotage it. So, I chill, get at them in the bed, it lasts as long as it does, and I move on."

B said, "Yeah, I'm not used to that, man. All I know is being with one woman."

D said, "I feel you, man. We all have to do us and be our best selves. Everything isn't for everybody. Yo, since we keep running into each other, and your ass is obviously not going to hit me up Mr. 'I want my own but I can't find anyone doing anything'"—D chuckled—"I'm going to invite you to a business summit that my boy is hosting. There is a private session on the same day in another part of the building. I'll get you in that and introduce you to some key players, man. But before that I need to see what you are working with as far as what you want to do. You got a plan?"

B said, "I haven't really worked it out yet, man. I want to do construction and have my own company. I want do real estate and I want to do public works projects."

D said, "That's a good overview, but you gone need more than that. I tell you what, conceptualize your ideas on paper. Watch some videos, do some hardcore research. If you need help, I got friends that can help."

B said, "Thanks, man. I appreciate it. I will do what I can and call you soon."

D replied, "Yeah, okay on that call shit. I'm fucking with you man."

B said, "Man, it's hard for me to trust people now man. I've been through a lot with folks."

D said, "Let me stop you right there. You think that I haven't? Man, this world showed me long ago that it couldn't give a fuck about what I think and feel. I don't worry about what people want or their opinions. I do what I do and people click with me or they don't. It's too many people, man. Too many opportunities. Life brings you what it brings you. It challenges you. To make you better. Let it make you better. Fuck what someone said or did to you. Determine what you're going to tolerate and what you're not. Let people go if they don't respect you. Move on. Trust me, there are people out here that will be what you need them to be. Bruh, peep this—this world and how it works is a game. Everyone ultimately is in this for themselves. You must be selfish sometimes. Hell, I'm selfish all the time. You won't hear me talking like you. Not to put you down. But you should stop expecting so much from people. Let them show you them and you do you. Part ways if you must. Your past that you hinted at before, it made you who you are, man. But it's behind you now. That milk is spilled. You are here now. What are you going to do now?"

B stood there, quiet and thinking deeply.

B at first thought that D was hard and uncaring but after hearing the dissertation that D had just given, B realized that D was calling out the man in him to man up and be responsible and move on. B then said, "You're right, man. I have to see this stuff differently and do differently."

D stated, "Look, man, get your business ideas together. Get at me. In two weeks is the business summit. Real shit, holler at me."

B replied, "No doubt, man. I will."

D gave B dap and they said their goodbyes and D left the bookstore. B grabbed a book on the ancient Maya, paid for it, and left the bookstore.

On a Wednesday, two weeks later, the business summit was held in the "Hot District." There were thousands of people there. B arrived and texted D to let him know that he was there. D texted him back and let him know that he should listen to the seminars, and that he would get him soon to come to the private session that was apparently going on while the main session was being held.

B intently listened to the speaker in the front as he walked the stage discussing business strategy and finances. B had always desired to be self-sufficient and self-reliant, but he hadn't the courage to take the step outside of working a 9-to-5 job. Eventually, after the third speaker and after 2 hours had passed, B had taken several notes, D texted B to guide him to the rear of the front stage.

As B walked along the west wall to the rear of the front stage, a large muscle-bound man approached him, greeted him, asked him who he was, and led him to the back. Apparently, D had already gotten in touch with the large man. As B made it to the door of the room where D and his business partners were, a young lady opened the door, and B walked in.

D introduced B to all his business partners, including the young lady that opened the door. The young lady and B locked eye contact for quite some time. She smiled, B smiled, and D noticed,

The discussion began. B presented his business plan and notes. D looked at the information that B provided while B began to explain in avid detail what his plans were and where he wanted to go. B had every intention of impressing this group of people, including D. Little did B know, D had already talked to his business partners about him and given them what he could as to where B wanted to go. D and B had a connection from the time they met in the coffee shop. It was as if they had met before in a previous life. D felt like a big brother to him, or perhaps an older version of B. D, too, had every intention of assisting B in his future business endeavors.

D and his business partners D were pleased with what they heard from B. They agreed to assist him in his endeavors. B decided to keep his day job while he worked his side business on the side. He would work nights and weekends on his business while working his day job. D and his business partners agreed with B that that would be ideal. They all shook hands and set up another meeting with regular meetings to follow. B was so pleased and thanked D over and over for helping him by hooking him up with his business partners and agreeing to assist him in his business goals.

Later, after the meeting, D pulled B to the side and asked him about the young lady who opened the door. "Bruh, I saw you looking at Sakaya. What you think, man?" asked D.

B said, "Man, I think that she is beautiful. Is she seeing anyone?"

D replied, "Naw, man. She was married for a few years. They never had children. She's a part of the group too, man. She only deals with guys who want to settle down and would be willing to be in something with her long-term. So, if you are interested, keep that in mind."

B said, "Man, I would be with her for the long-term. What is she like?"

D said, "Bruh, I'm going to introduce you to her. She is good people, man. She got her own money, and she knows what she wants. For her to lock eyes with you like that, I believe shows that the feeling is mutual."

B was ecstatic about meeting Sakaya. D introduced them to one another. B asked her to take a walk so that they can go somewhere and talk. She agreed.

Six months later, after talking over the phone and a few dates, B decided to ask her to be with him long-term as his girlfriend and hinted to her that he would be interested in marrying her. She was so excited that she answered yes immediately after he asked her. Now B had gotten his business off the ground as he worked it on the side. B had gotten his, as it would seem, dream girl to agree to be his girl long-term. B was happier than he had ever been. B was seeing his stronger, brighter future.

Life is full of complexity, paradoxes, and hardship. Sometimes life starts out great for some and ends up horribly. Sometimes life starts out great for some and ends great. Sometimes life starts out bad and remains bad until the end. Sometimes life starts out bad and ends well. As the old saying goes, "Your latter is better than your former." For B, or Ben, much like Isaiah and the other old sages in what they wrote, the saying fits to a T. B's latter did indeed end up better than his former days.

ABOUT THE AUTHOR

Benjamin Samuel Brasford lived a relatively normal life, though he went through some major changes and battles in the beginning stages of his adulthood. After having been involved in an immediate family situation for a long time, he finally was able to free himself and begin to live life on his own terms. During the latter period of that immediate family situation, leading from just before its dissolution, Ben began doing research in an effort to learn about and understand life, beginning from where he was mentally at the time, Christianity. His Christian studies led to a broader approach to life in general. After years of time, effort, situations, and application, Ben decided to write about what he had learned with a desire to assist others in their journey. This volume is an introduction to a series of works that will demonstrate Ben's exploration. This narrative was for the purpose of introducing readers to what led Ben to become a student of life. Because of the later material that will be much broader but more in-depth, we thought that it was necessary to introduce you to the person by way of providing some background since Ben did not attend university for scholarly studies. Ben will continue learning, exploring and writing in the future on many of these same subject matters, as well as others not expressly stated within the current work. Please feel free to visit the following links, if you desire to follow Ben to remain aware of his current and future developments.

Blog: https://www.theworkseries.com/

Twitter: https://twitter.com/Brasford17

Academic Website: https://independent.academia.edu/BenjaminBrasford

www.ingramcontent.com/pod-product-compliance
Lightning Source LLC
Chambersburg PA
CBHW070943120726

47908CB00005BA/1509